Monty
The
Webless Spider

Written by
Heather Taylor-King

Illustrated by:
Uliana Barabash

Monty The Webless Spider

Author: Heather Taylor-King
Illustrator: Uliana Barabash
Editor: Russell Webb
Interior Design: hDigitals Design Studio

For Isla

Monty is a very special spider,

Not just because he is small and sweet,

He is special because he can't build a web,

Not even with his eight, hairy feet.

He has no room to rest his head,

To lay down after a busy day,

Nowhere to put his clothes and hats,

Or to store his shoes away.

Monty tried so many places,

Somewhere to call his own,

He wanted somewhere cosy,

To call his home sweet home.

One night he tried out a shoe,

That was left by the back door,

It was horribly smelly, Monty stayed one night,

He couldn't stay one more.

He climbed up high to the corner of the room,

It offered an amazing view,

But he learned he had a fear of heights,

So, he climbed back down – PHEW!

He then crept under the sofa,

It was dark and quiet, very nice!

But it was far too dusty and dirty,

Poor Monty left after sneezing twice.

Feeling very sad Monty, began to cry,

There was nowhere left to go,

When a girl's tiny voice spoke,

"Oh, little spider, I can help you, you know".

"I have the perfect place for you",

"It is safe, warm and dry",

"You can stay there for as long as you like",

"Oh, little spider, please don't cry".

Slowly the girl opened her hand,

In her palm there laid,

A little matchbox, covered in glitter,

Lined with cotton, edges frayed.

"This can be yours, if you would like",

The small, sweet girl kindly said",

So, in Monty quickly jumped,

Settling down, ready for bed.

Looking around he couldn't believe it,

A place to call his own,

I've even gained a friend, he thought,

Now, I'm no longer alone!

Feeling sleepy Monty closed his eyes,

There was nowhere left to roam,

At last, thought Monty with a sigh,

I have finally found my Home Sweet Home.